Praise for
Connor the Courageous Cutter

Connor is not only courageous, he's cute, calm, capable, and clever! Boating fans, their kids and grandkids will enjoy this exciting story that brings the ocean and its ocean-going cohorts to life!

—Kim Norman,
children's book author of
Ten on the Sled and *The Bot that Scott Built*

Your kids will love this book. Mine did.

—Del Wilber,
father of two

The *Connor the Courageous Cutter* book series is a great addition to our home and school libraries. Most importantly, they are proof that hope and positivity are still alive in children's literature!

—Jenelle Mejia,
teacher and mother of five

To Jax and Nugget. Always remember…man who catch fly with chopstick accomplish anything. To Connor, Gray, Tristan, and Dez. May these adventures spark your imaginations and inspire you to follow your dreams. To my loving wife April. Thank you for being my beacon, my anchor, and my safe harbor.

-Scott

To Mom, Dad, Michelle, Heather, and India. No matter how many stories I tell, or characters I bring to life, the prologue to everything I know will always begin with the crazy Thompson family from Sheffield Lake, Ohio. Never forget that Nancy and Ronald Reagan once had a baby…and it had wrinkles.

-Rod

www.mascotbooks.com

The Adventures of Connor the Courageous Cutter: Caution At Calamity Canal

For more information, please contact:
Mascot Books
560 Herndon Parkway #120
Herndon, VA 20170
info@mascotbooks.com

Library of Congress Control Number: 2016910836

The Adventures Of

CONNOR THE COURAGEOUS CUTTER

Caution At Calamity Canal

by Scott McBride & Rodger Thompson

Illustrated by Brian Martin

Journey with me to a place far away,
Across the seas, and beyond the bays.

Through the big river basins, and just past the capes,
There's a place full of boats of all sizes and shapes.

Come hear their tales, come gather 'round.
And take a voyage with me, to Serendipity Sound!

- Anna the Lighthouse

It was a beautiful, busy morning around Serendipity Sound. Here, there, and everywhere, boats shuffled about their daily routines.

Barry the Barge unloaded coal from his trip to Blackwood Bay, while Sarah the Schooner trained a new class of junior sailboats how to race. Grayson the Tug-N-Tow pushed a heavy load of freshly cut timber through the sound and Felipe the Fishing Trawler prepared his nets.

Everything seemed perfectly normal, yet, something fishy was in the air, and it wasn't just the smell of Felipe's nets.

In the channel, Faith was leading Connor out to sea.

As they passed Anna the Lighthouse, she beamed down on them with a smile. “Hello, Faith. Hello, Connor. Where are you headed today?”

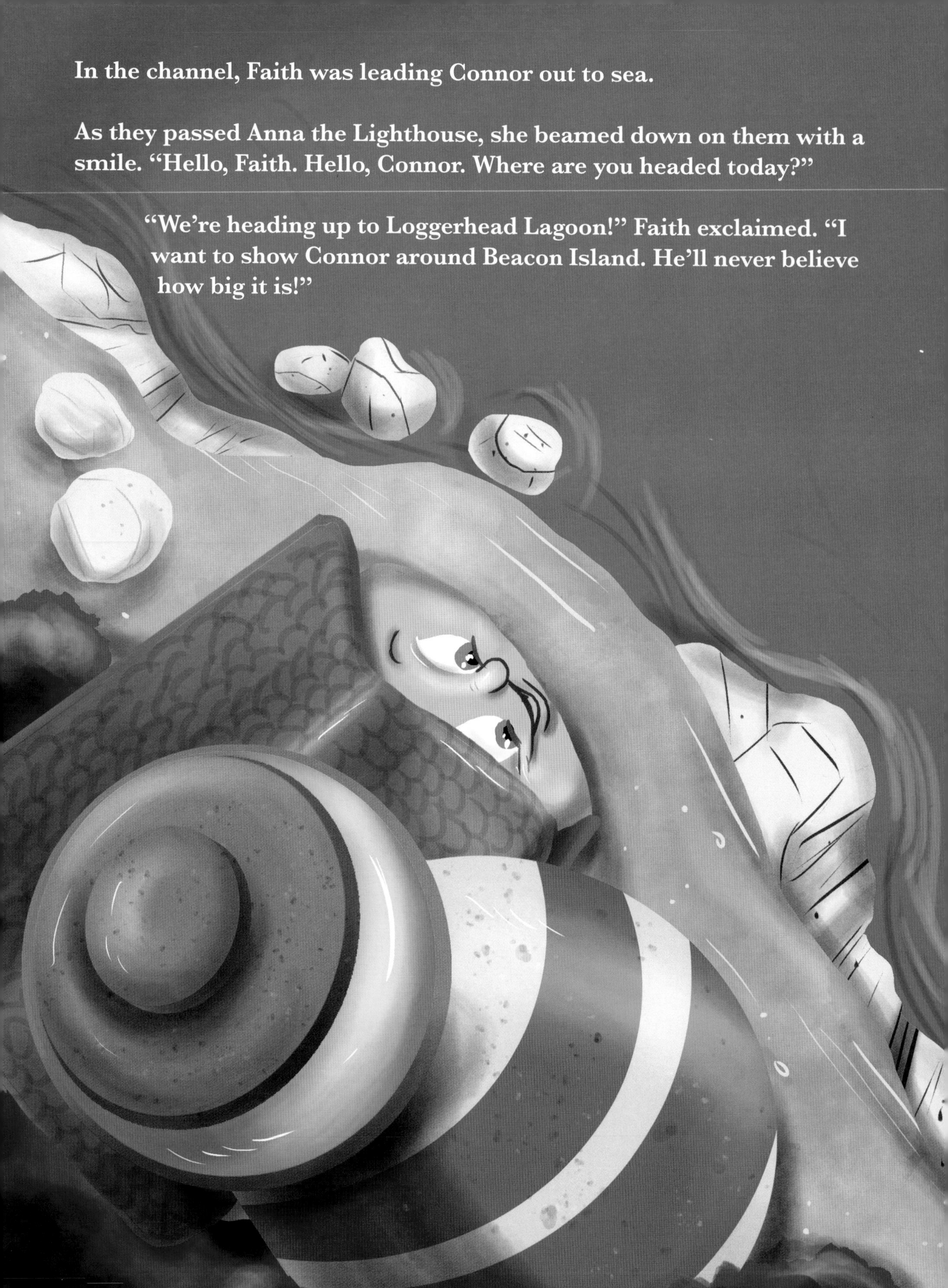

“We’re heading up to Loggerhead Lagoon!” Faith exclaimed. “I want to show Connor around Beacon Island. He’ll never believe how big it is!”

Beyond Serendipity Sound, there were many ports, bays, coves, and rivers where other boats lived happily, but Connor, being one of the newest residents, had yet to visit them.

Anna scanned around in all directions. “Weather looks clear for miles and miles. You two be safe,” she called down.

“Yes ma’am, we will,” Connor yelled back. “Safety always comes first when Connor the Cutter is around!”

The two boats turned northward and passed Pickles the Sea Buoy with a toot of their whistles as they began their journey to Loggerhead Lagoon.

Back in Serendipity Sound, Naomi the News Chopper watched Faith and Connor from high in the sky. Once she was sure that they were gone, she swooped down to the other boats.

"Are they gone?" Grayson the Tug-N-Tow asked.

"Yessirrrrrendipity, they are! Moving with the tides. Rolling with the waves," Naomi exclaimed.

All of the boats hustled about, gathering party decorations. Ribbons, streamers, and balloons were taped, tied, and tacked to everything that was bolted down.

“What’s all this fuss about anyway?” asked Thaddeus.

“It’s for Connor’s welcoming party, silly!” replied Sarah the Schooner.

“Parties aren’t good for nothing but noise and making a mess,” Thaddeus huffed before dozing back off into his nap.

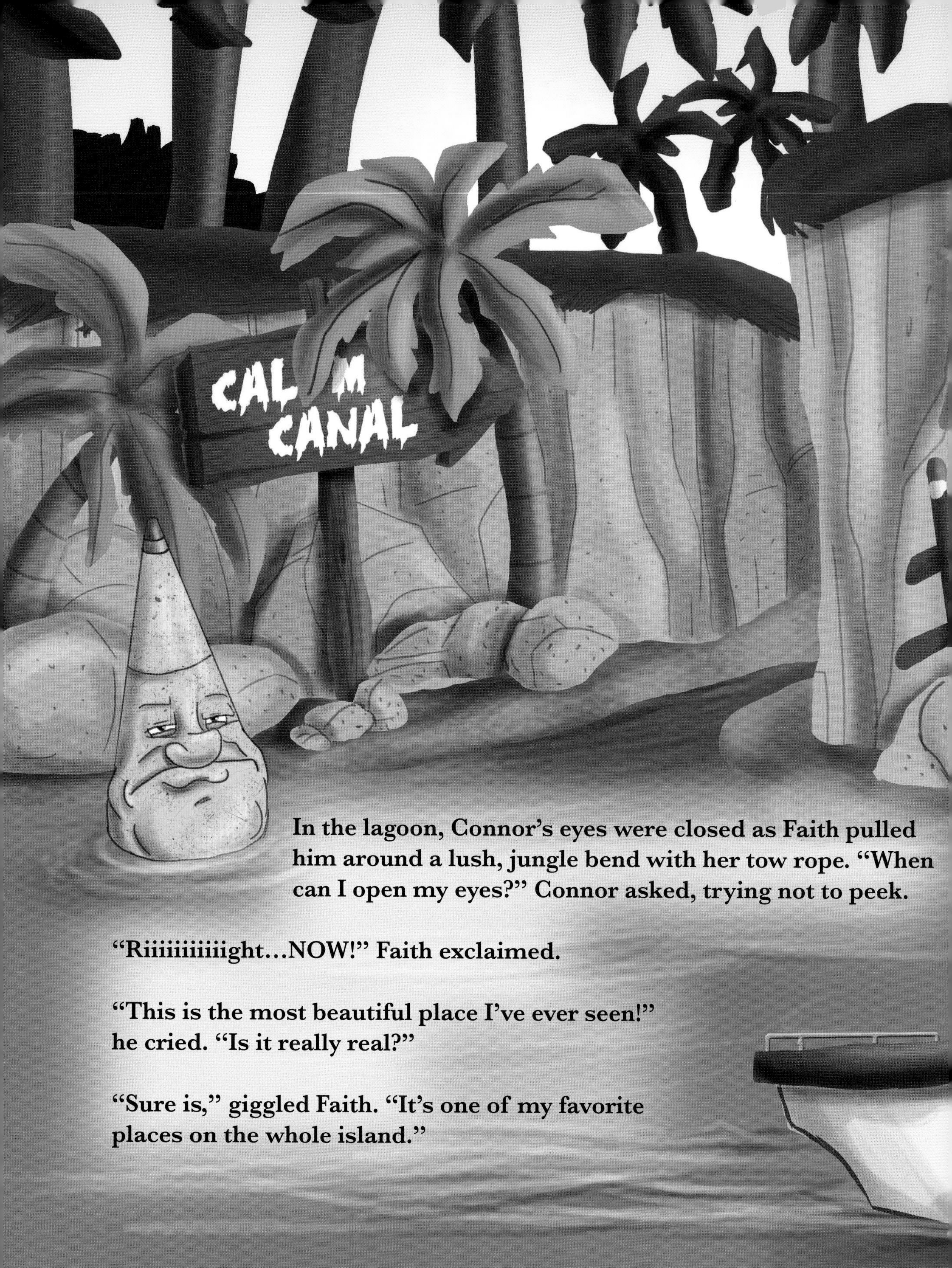

In the lagoon, Connor's eyes were closed as Faith pulled him around a lush, jungle bend with her tow rope. "When can I open my eyes?" Connor asked, trying not to peek.

"Riiiiiiiiiiight…NOW!" Faith exclaimed.

"This is the most beautiful place I've ever seen!" he cried. "Is it really real?"

"Sure is," giggled Faith. "It's one of my favorite places on the whole island."

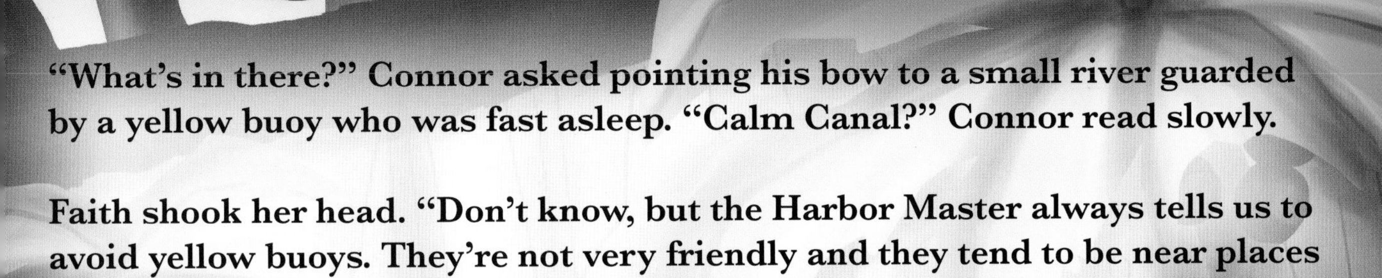

"What's in there?" Connor asked pointing his bow to a small river guarded by a yellow buoy who was fast asleep. "Calm Canal?" Connor read slowly.

Faith shook her head. "Don't know, but the Harbor Master always tells us to avoid yellow buoys. They're not very friendly and they tend to be near places that might be dangerous for boats. Come on, let's finish the tour!"

Connor looked back as they kept moving along. *Odd,* he thought, *it doesn't look very dangerous over there.*

As they finished up the tour, Faith looked up to the sun and suddenly realized she'd lost track of time. They were going to be late for Connor's surprise party!

"Oh no! Connor! We have to go," Faith said.

The yellow buoy opened its eyes. "You gonna be late, kid? Take the canal. It's a shortcut."

Faith shook her bow, "No way! The Harbor Master says we're not supposed to listen to yellow buoys."

"You kiddin' me?" the yellow buoy said with a smirk. "Canals are made for boats. Trust me. I know the Harbor Master personally, and if he wants you back at a certain time, he ain't gonna get mad at you for taking a shortcut."

CALAMITY
CANAL

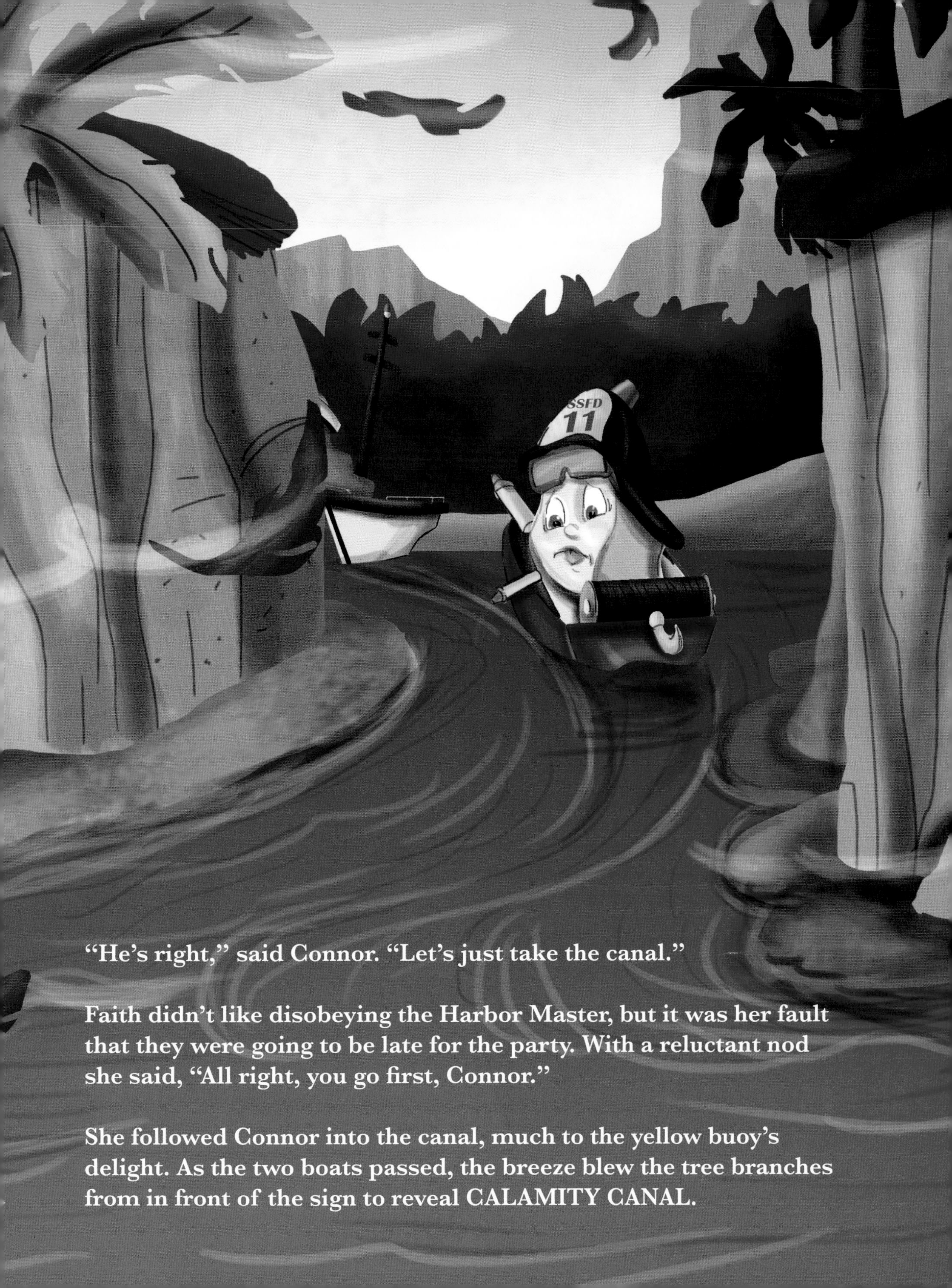

"He's right," said Connor. "Let's just take the canal."

Faith didn't like disobeying the Harbor Master, but it was her fault that they were going to be late for the party. With a reluctant nod she said, "All right, you go first, Connor."

She followed Connor into the canal, much to the yellow buoy's delight. As the two boats passed, the breeze blew the tree branches from in front of the sign to reveal CALAMITY CANAL.

The small canal wound left and right like a serpent, thick with thorny tree branches and sharp rocks on both sides. As the jungle grew darker, Calamity Canal became scarier and scarier.

"Ouch!" Connor exclaimed. "These tree branches are prickly."

"I can't see around the next bend! I'm scared, Connor," Faith said with a shiver.

"I am too, but it's too tight to turn around. We have to keep going."

"I don't like this adventure at all," said Faith, growing angry with herself. She knew that the Harbor Master had told all of the boats to never talk to caution buoys, and now she knew why.

In Serendipity Sound, the party decorations were up and everyone was waiting for Connor and Faith to arrive. Naomi flew high above but saw no sign of them.

“Where are they already?” Yardly the Yacht huffed. “I haven’t the time to simply wait. It’s nearly time for tea.”

"Oh, Yardly. You can miss your tea just this once. We're here to celebrate Connor," Sarah said with a huge smile.

"My dear, there are few things in this world more important than tea time, and I can assure you that this is not one of them," Yardly said with his bow pointed upward.

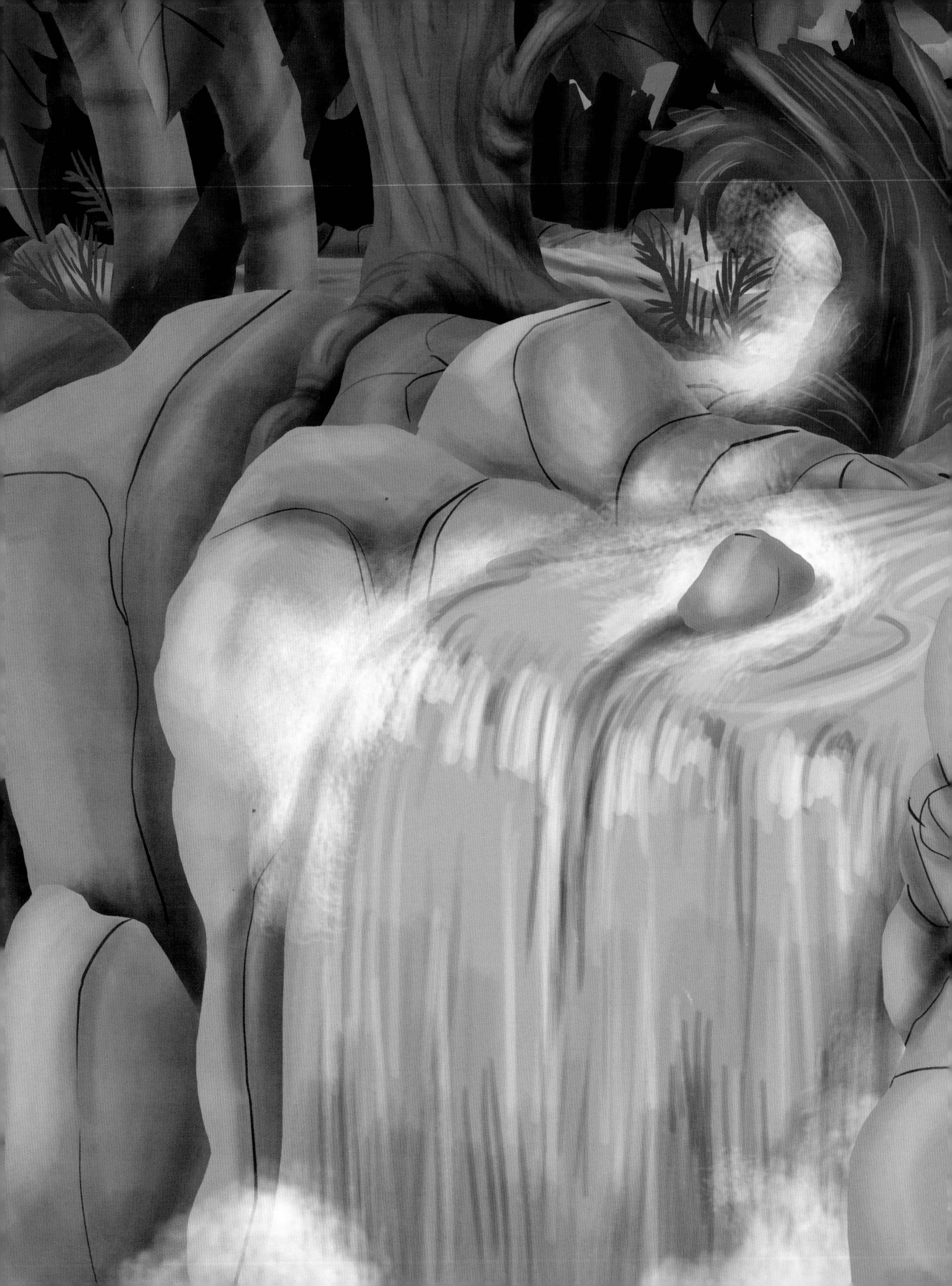

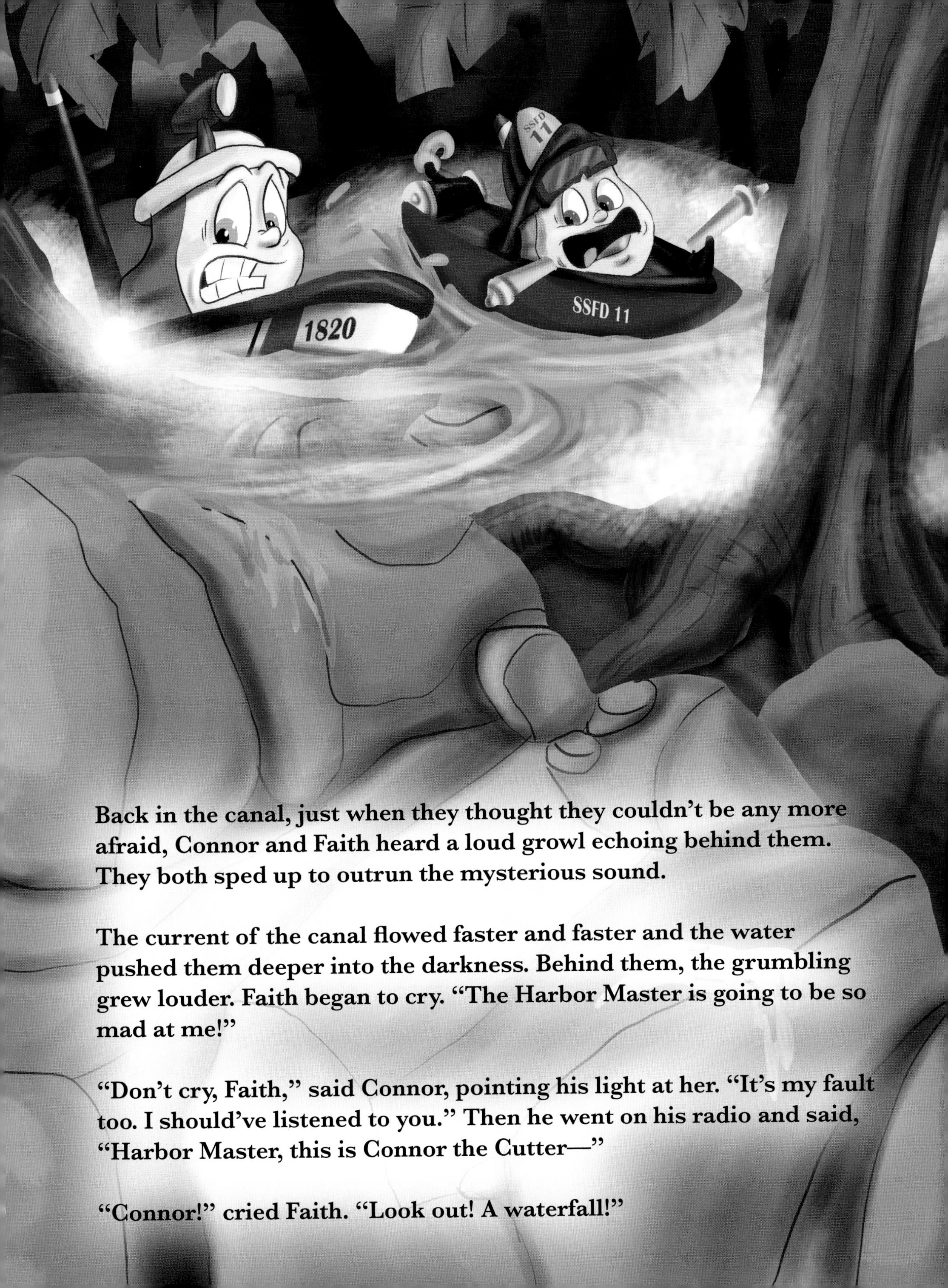

Back in the canal, just when they thought they couldn't be any more afraid, Connor and Faith heard a loud growl echoing behind them. They both sped up to outrun the mysterious sound.

The current of the canal flowed faster and faster and the water pushed them deeper into the darkness. Behind them, the grumbling grew louder. Faith began to cry. "The Harbor Master is going to be so mad at me!"

"Don't cry, Faith," said Connor, pointing his light at her. "It's my fault too. I should've listened to you." Then he went on his radio and said, "Harbor Master, this is Connor the Cutter—"

"Connor!" cried Faith. "Look out! A waterfall!"

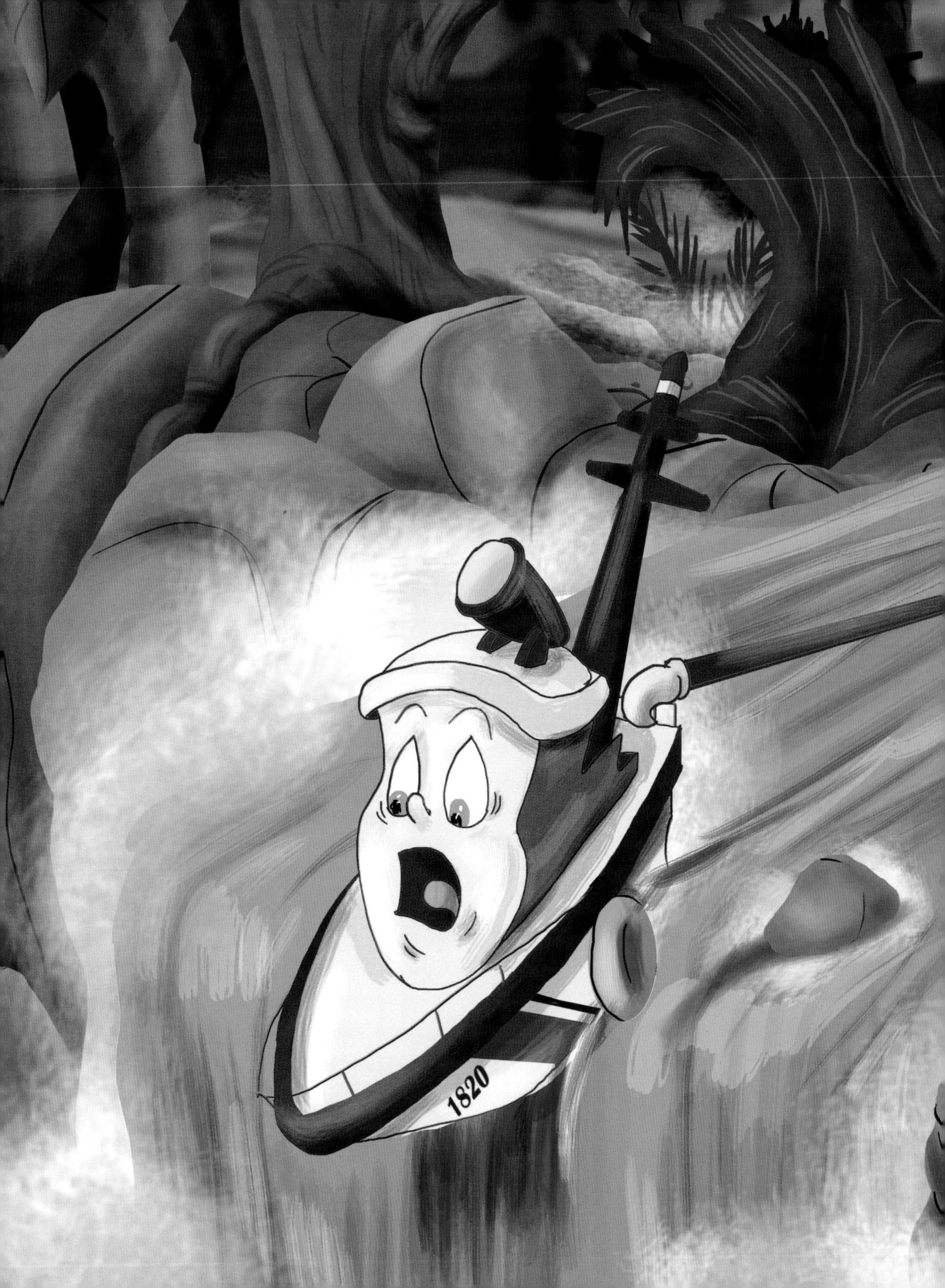
1820

Connor and Faith reversed their engines, but the force of the water pulled them toward the falls. Faith shot her tow line over to Connor and pulled as hard as she could.

"Oh no, I'm going over!" Connor yelled, getting closer and closer to the tremendous drop beneath him.

Faith shot another tow line to a nearby tree and pulled, but the tree started to bend. It would only be a matter of time before it broke and sent her and Connor to the bottom of the falls. As her engines started to smoke, the tree made a popping sound, and the growling behind them turned into a deafening mechanical thunder! When all of a sudden…

SNA
SSFD 11
SSFD 11

Grayson the Tug-N-Tow's lines hooked into Faith's stern, just as the tree gave way.

"I gotcha, Faith!" shouted Grayson as he used his two colossal, rumbling diesel engines to pull them up from the falls. "Come on, let's get out of here!"

Connor and Faith thanked Grayson from the bottom of their keels for saving them. Grayson smiled, out of breath, and replied, "Thank the Harbor Master. He's the one that told me where to find you. I'm just glad I caught up to you in time!"

It was dark by the time Connor and Faith returned to the sound, and Anna beamed her light down on them. "You two okay?"

Faith looked away. "Is the Harbor Master mad?"

"Mad? Why would the Harbor Master be mad?" Anna asked.

"Because we listened to the yellow buoy and disobeyed him," Connor replied.

"Oh, the Harbor Master doesn't get mad. He may be disappointed you didn't follow his rules, but he'll forgive you. Once he saw you were in trouble on his radar, he sent Grayson right away to bring you home. Does that sound like he was mad at you? Sometimes taking shortcuts might seem like an easier path, but it may not always have the best result."

"Yes, ma'am," Connor said. In the distance, he heard music echoing from the sound.

Anna looked towards the piers, "Faith, my darlin', don't you have somewhere to take Connor?"

With a small smile breaking her sadness, Faith bumped Connor. "Come on, Connor. I've got something to show you."

Coming around the bend, scratched and dinged up, Connor was shocked with happiness as he looked at the piers and saw all of the boats in Serendipity Sound floating near his berth. Streamers, balloons, and lights were strung from pier to pier, and dock to dock.

And all of the boats shouted together, "Welcome home, Connor!"

WELCOME CONNOR

ABOUT THE AUTHORS

About Scott

A native of McLean, Virginia, Scott McBride became inspired to write children's books while attending graduate school at the University of North Carolina at Chapel Hill. As a husband and father of two boys, he felt called to share fun and exciting morality-based stories with positive messages to both adults and children. His stories focus on things he truly loves: the Lord, boats, and the sea. He hopes both kids and parents alike find joy and happiness as they share in the adventures that wait for Connor and his friends in Serendipity Sound. Scott is a 1998 graduate of the United States Naval Academy and holds a Masters Degree in Mass Communication from the UNC School of Media and Journalism. Scott is a Navy veteran and currently serves on active duty in the U.S. Coast Guard. Welcome aboard!

About Rod

The youngest child of the nomadic Thompson clan, Rod has been writing creatively since he first learned that "words can create worlds." A seasoned screenwriter of over ten years, he enjoys the cinematic approach to storytelling, and has celebrated numerous competition successes as well as produced films from scripts he has written. He is unshakably devoted to God, his wife, and to making sure that his three sons understand what it means to be a "good man." Rod currently serves in his seventeenth year on active duty with the U.S. Navy, is a dedicated public servant, and attends film school at Regent University.